COALITION OF MALICE

STEVE YOUNG
COVER ARTIST

CHRISTOPHER MEYER
EDITOR

SPECIAL THANKS TO LYNNE KARPPI, DANIELLE GILLIS, AND GARY HYMOWITZ

For information regarding the CPSIA on this printed material, call: (203) 595-3636 and provide reference #EAST – 384140. A catalog record of this book is available from OCLC and from the KABOOM! website, www.kaboom-studios.com, on the Librarians Page.

BOOM! Studios, 6310 San Vicente Boulevard, Suite 107, Los Angeles, CA 90048-5457. Printed in USA. First Printing. ISBN: 978-1-60886-678-6

COALITION OF MALICE

Chris Karwowski
WRITER

Steve Young
ART AND COLORS

Jason Arthur
LETTERS

THIS NORMAL-LOOKING BUT EXHAUSTED GIRL IS BECKY BOTSFORD. TO MOST PEOPLE, SHE'S AN AVERAGE 5TH GRADER WITH A BETTER-THAN-AVERAGE VOCABULARY.
BUT IF YOU CAN KEEP A SECRET, I'LL TELL YOU THAT SHE IS ALSO...
WORDGIRL™
SUPER-POWERED HERO FROM THE PLANET LEXICON! WHO, ALONG WITH HER SIDEKICK, CAPTAIN HUGGY FACE, FIGHTS FOR TRUTH, JUSTICE, AND USE OF THE RIGHT WORD!
(FORGIVE ME IF I GET A LITTLE GIDDY. I JUST THINK WORDGIRL IS NEAT.)

LATELY, WORDGIRL'S BEEN BUSIER THAN EVER.
BUT WHO COULD BLAME HER?

WHAT A WEEK, HUGGY! I CAN'T WAIT TO GET SOME SLEEP.
OOOO.
BEEP BEEP BEEP
C'MON, BOB. LET'S GET TO THE WATERFRONT ALREADY.
yawn

eeeeeh
ALL THAT WORK AND NO SLEEP HAS MADE ME EXHAUSTED, TOO.
HUH. LOOKS LIKE NOBODY'S HERE.
WELL, AT LEAST NOW WE CAN CATCH SOME SLEEP...OR GET AN EARLY START ON MY HISTORY ESSAY!
NO SUCH LUCK FOR YOU, WORDGIRL! BECAUSE TODAY, YOU FACE...

THE COALITION OF MALICE!
DR. TWO-BRAINS
MR. BIG
THE BUTCHER
GRANNY MAY
CHUCK THE EVIL SANDWICH MAKING GUY

WAIT...A COALITION? FIVE OF MY ARCH-ENEMIES JOINED TOGETHER?
I MEAN, WHY ARE YOU GUYS EVEN TEAMING UP? DO WE HAVE TO FIGHT SO EARLY IN THE MORNING? AND HOW DID YOU MAKE THE WORDGIRL ALARM GO OFF?
DOES WORDGIRL ASK THIS MANY QUESTIONS WHEN YOU GUYS FIGHT HER?
I DON'T THINK SO.
NOT USUALLY.
I'M SORRY, I'M JUST EXHAUSTED.
WHAT DOES WORDGIRL BEING EGG-TOASTED HAVE TO DO WITH ANYTHING?
OH, GREAT.
YOU BIG OAF, BUTCHER!
WHAT? WHAT DID I DO WRONG?

NOW WORDGIRL IS GOING TO DEFINE WHAT EXHAUSTED MEANS.
SHE DOES DO STUFF LIKE THAT.
YES, I KNOW.
YOU'RE RIGHT. EXHAUSTED MEANS BEING VERY, VERY TIRED. TO THE POINT WHERE ALL OF YOUR ENERGY IS DEPLETED.
EXHAUSTED OR NOT, YOU'VE GOT YOUR WORK CUT OUT FOR YOU! BECAUSE WE HAVE JOINED FORCES TO DEFEAT YOU AND ROB THIS TOWN BLIND!
BY OURSELVES, WE ALWAYS SEEM TO LOSE TO YOU AND YOUR ARMADILLO FRIEND THERE...

"...BUT, AT THE LAST VILLAINS ASSOCIATION MEETING, WE RAISED THE QUESTION: WHAT IF WE JOINED FORCES AS A *COALITION?*"
YOU'RE NOT TELLING HER THE BEST PART, WHIPPER-SNAPPER!
OH YES, WELL, AFTER WE DEFEAT YOU, WE'RE GOING TO *UNMASK* YOU AND LEARN YOUR SECRET IDENTITY. WITHOUT THAT, YOU'LL BE COMPLETELY AT OUR MERCY!
IT'S THE *PERFECT PLAN!*
HA HA
HA HA
HA HA HA HA HA
UH... WORDGIRL?
HEY! SHE CAN'T DO THIS TO US!
ZZZZZ

WORDGIRL... FELL ASLEEP?
WHY I NEVER!
I TOLD YOU TO KEEP THE ORIGIN STORY SHORT.
THAT WAS THE SHORT VERSION. I DIDN'T EVEN TELL HER ABOUT THE SNACKS.
THOSE CHEESE PUFFS WERE TASTY.
ENOUGH! LET'S TAKE OFF THE SHRIMP'S HOOD AND BE DONE WITH IT.

YOU KNOW, THAT DON'T SEEM SO SPORKMAN-LIKE TO ME.
YEAH, IT JUST FEELS...WHAT'S THE WORD...I JUST HAD IT...
WEIRD?
SNEAKY?
UNSPORKMAN-LIKE?
ARE WE REALLY GOING TO LISTEN TO THIS BREAD-HEADED BUFFOON?
HEY! WHEN WE FORMED THE COALITION OF MALICE, WE AGREED TO BE NICE TO EACH OTHER.
WELL WE ALSO AGREED TO UNMASK THIS CRIME FIGHTING DO-GOODER!
YES! SHE ALWAYS STOPS ME FROM STEALING CHEESE, AND HURTS MY HENCHMEN. MOUSE BRAIN SAYS UNMASK HER!
YEAH, BUT... THIS AIN'T THE WAY TO DO IT.
IT JUST SEEMS...UH... SNEAKY! THAT'S WHAT I WAS TRYING TO THINK OF.
I SAID SNEAKY!
OH, SORRY. I DIDN'T HEAR YOU.

Butcher, Chuck... don't you want to be *free?* To live in a world where WordGirl won't foil your plans anymore?
WELL... WELL, *YEAH,* BUT...
Then *surely* you wouldn't prevent a nice old lady from unmasking her *greatest enemy?*
I JUST THINK WE SHOULD GIVE HER A FIGHTING CHANCE.
YEAH!
I DIDN'T KNOW YOU FELT SO STRONGLY.
IN THAT CASE...

...LET'S FIGHT IT OUT, MEAT MAN!
IT'S ON, LITTLE LADY!
EVERYONE, PLEASE!
THERE'S NO NEED TO FIGHT AMONGST OURSELVES.
YOU KNOW, MY ASSISTANT LESLIE TOLD ME TO USE MIND CONTROL ON ALL OF YOU.
BUT I TOLD HER NO, THAT I WAS DEALING WITH PROFESSIONALS. NOT AMATEURS. YOU DON'T NEED THE MIND CONTROL RAY FOR PROFESSIONALS, I TOLD HER.
SO, IN CLOSING, BE PROFESSIONAL. OR I WILL HAVE TO PULL OUT THE RAY.

SKRONK!
WORDGIRL! STOP!

I IMAGINE YOU ARE CONFUSED, BUT THERE IS NO NEED FOR VIOLENCE. I SWEAR TO YOU, MY ROBOTS AND I ARE INNOCENT.

TOBEY, NO ONE WITH A ROBOT ARMY IS EVER INNOCENT.
TRUE...
THIS BETTER NOT BE PART OF THE COALITION OF MALICE'S PLAN, OR I'M TURNING YOUR FRIENDS INTO SCRAP METAL.

MY MY, WORDGIRL. MUST YOU FEEL THIS WAY TOWARDS THE BRILLIANT AND HANDSOME PERSON WHO SAVED YOU FROM THE COALITION'S CLUTCHES? PERHAPS I SHOULD TELL YOU THE WHOLE STORY...
HERE WE GO...

"I WAS AT THE MEETING WHEN THE COALITION OF MALICE FORMED. THEY CALLED THEMSELVES YOUR *GREATEST ENEMIES!* HA! *I* AM YOUR GREATEST ENEMY. BUT...

"...THOSE *CORRUPT* SNOBS REJECTED ME.
"SO BE IT! I DON'T NEED THEM ANYWAY."

"I OVERHEARD THEIR PLANS, SO I DECIDED THAT IF I COULDN'T JOIN THEM, AT LEAST I COULD *FOIL* THEM.
"BUT HOW? I COULD NOT ATTACK THEM DIRECTLY, ACCORDING TO THE VILLAIN CODE OF CONDUCT.

"YOUR INSPIRED STRATEGY OF FALLING ASLEEP ON THEM GAVE MY ROBOT ENOUGH TIME TO SNATCH YOU RIGHT OUT FROM UNDER THEIR *CORRUPT* NOSES."
"UH, *STRATEGY*... RIGHT..."

AND PLEASE DON'T DEFINE *CORRUPT*. *I* ALREADY KNOW WHAT IT MEANS.
FINE. BUT I'M BETTING IT *WILL* BE DEFINED BEFORE ALL IS SAID AND DONE.
I GUESS WE SHALL SEE.
I GUESS WE SHALL.

"CORRUPT"... HMM.
TOBEY, DOES YOUR CODE OF CONDUCT PREVENT YOU FROM WEARING A FAKE MOUSTACHE?
...I'M LISTENING...

"DEAR CHUCK THE EVIL SANDWICH MAKING GUY, LET'S DITCH THE COALITION OF MALICE AND BECOME A TWO-MAN CRIME TEAM. TOGETHER, WE COULD RULE THIS CITY.
"P.S. DON'T TELL...
"...ANYONE ELSE..."
OH, HELLO...
FANCY MEETING YOU HERE.
HIYA...
WOW, THIS IS AWKWARD...

WHAT IS GOING ON HERE?! I CAME HERE TO TEAM UP WITH MR. BIG. NOT TO LOOK AT YOUR UGLY MUGS.

BUT I WAS SUPPOSED TO MEET WITH DOCTOR TWO-BRAINS...WHO, I FELT, WOULD MAKE A BETTER PARTNER. NO OFFENSE.
TWO-BRAINS?

I DON'T SEE WHY THAT EGG-HEAD IS SO GREAT.
I'M NOT AN *EGG-HEAD*. I'M AN *EVIL MOUSE-HEAD!* AND PROUD OF IT!

WAIT! GRANNY, I THOUGHT *YOU* AND *ME* WAS SUPPOSED TO BE A *COALMISSION.*
BUTCHER, WHAT POSSIBLE USE WOULD I HAVE FOR A MAN WHO CAN SHOOT *MEAT* OUT OF HIS HANDS?

ARE YOU KIDDING? THE BUTCHER IS AWESOME. THAT'S WHY I WAS SO EXCITED TO JOIN FORCES WITH HIM.
YEAH... UH, ABOUT THAT...
I'LL TEAM UP WITH YOU, CHUCK.
I DON'T KNOW, DOCTOR. I DON'T REALLY NEED THAT MUCH CHEESE.
HMMPH. IT WAS JUST A PITY PARTNERSHIP ANYWAY.
WELL, THAT'S JUST RUDE! BUTCHER, TAKE HIM OUT!
EVERYONE, CALM DOWN!
I AIN'T YOUR PARTNER, CHUCK. I'M TEAMING UP WITH GRANNY MAY.
THE DEVIL YOU ARE! MR. BIG, SHUT YOUR THINK-HOLE AND LET'S GO DO SOME CRIME!
WHY IS EVERYONE BEING SO MEAN?!
ARGH! MOUSE BRAIN IS CONFUSED!
I HAVE HAD IT UP TO HERE WITH YOU WHINY VILLAINS! AMATEURS. I CALL YOU AMATEURS!

YOU SEE? NEVER UNDERESTIMATE THE POWER OF PASSING NOTES.
HUGGY, I THINK IT'S TIME TO KICK THIS FIGHT INTO HIGH GEAR!

HEY...

GOTCHA!
POW! POW!

OOPS.
SEE... THE THING IS...
UH...

HYAH! HYAH!
HAVE AT YOU!
HA HA HA HA HA!
PASTRAMI ATTACK!
TASTE MY MUSTARD!

NICE WORK, HUGGY!

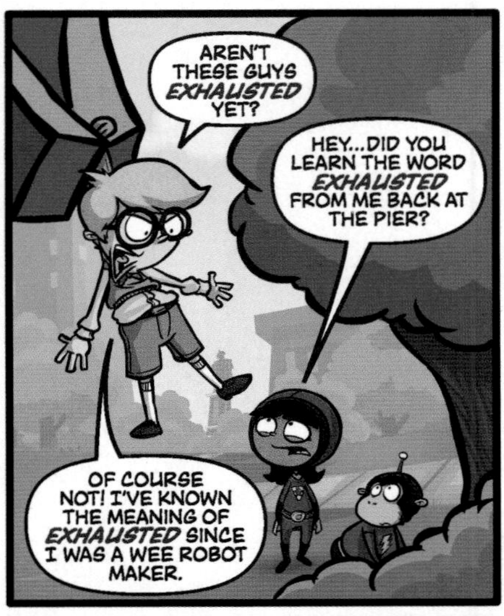
AREN'T THESE GUYS EXHAUSTED YET?
HEY...DID YOU LEARN THE WORD EXHAUSTED FROM ME BACK AT THE PIER?
OF COURSE NOT! I'VE KNOWN THE MEANING OF EXHAUSTED SINCE I WAS A WEE ROBOT MAKER.

TOBEY, CAN YOU HOLD THIS ROPE?
I TOLD YOU, I CAN'T BE DIRECTLY INVOLVED.
WELL... CAN YOU HAVE YOUR ROBOT HOLD IT?
...I SUPPOSE.

WHAT ARE YOU GOING TO DO?
WRAP THIS UP IN A PRETTY BOW.
WORD UP!

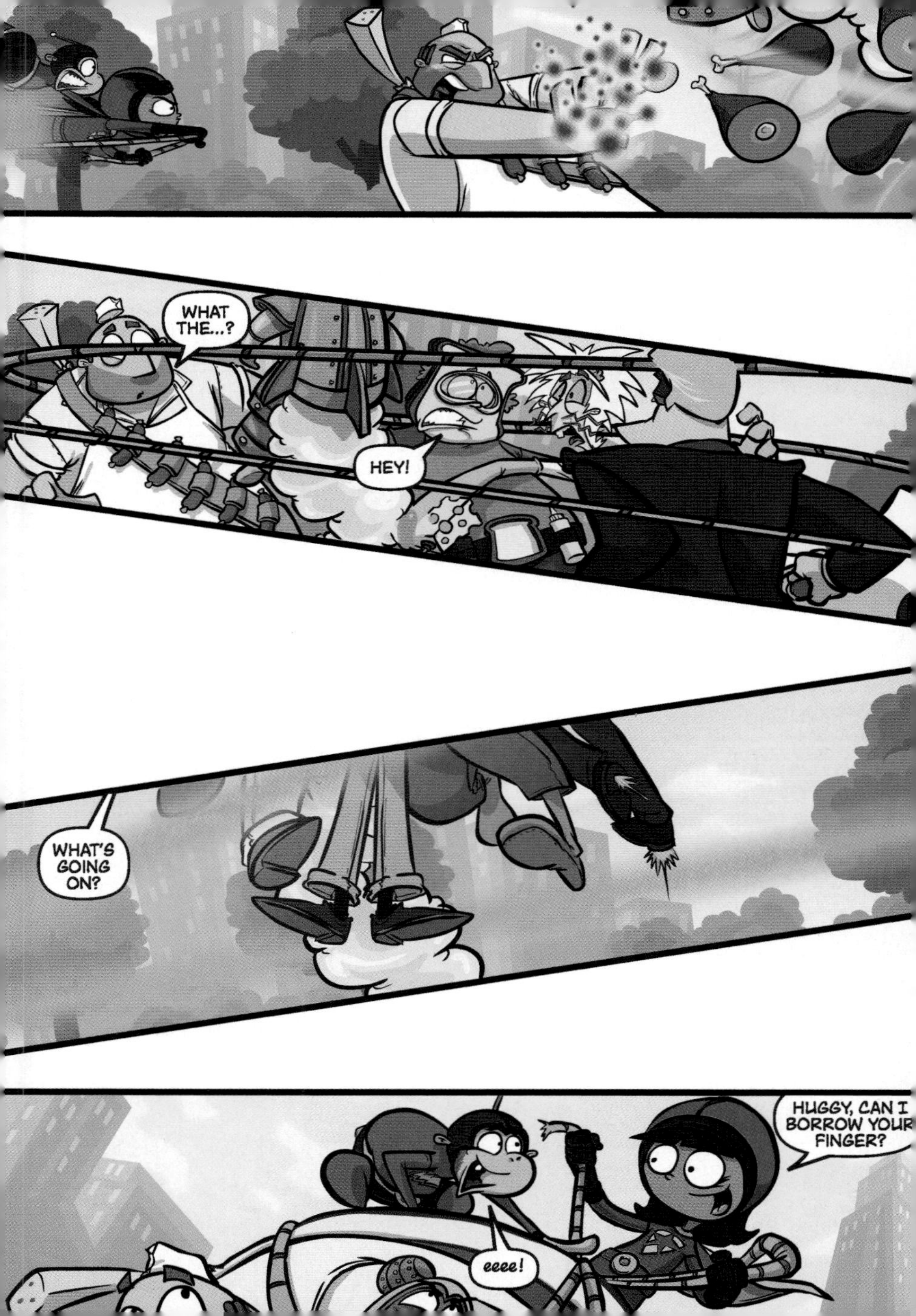
WHAT THE...?
HEY!
WHAT'S GOING ON?
HUGGY, CAN I BORROW YOUR FINGER?
eeee!

TA-DA!
WORDGIRL!
OH NO!
WE'VE BEEN DUPED!
YOU SEE? THIS IS WHY VILLAINS DON'T WORK TOGETHER. YOU GUYS HAVE SERIOUS TRUST ISSUES.
I HEAR YOU LOUD AND CLEAR, WORDGIRL. THE COALITION OF MALICE IS NO MORE.
NO ARGUMENTS HERE.
WE'LL JUST BE ON OUR WAY, THEN.
YEAH, JUST UNTIRE US.
FIRST, IT'S UNTIE. SECOND, I DON'T THINK SO. THE POLICE WANT TO TALK TO YOU ABOUT DISTURBING THE PEACE.
THEY ALSO ROBBED THREE BANKS AND A PIZZA PARLOR TODAY.
OH. THAT TOO.

OFFICER, TAKE THESE CRIMINALS AWAY!
TOBEY? YOU *TEAMED UP* WITH WORDGIRL?! THAT IS AGAINST HALF THE RULES OF THE VILLAINS ASSOCIATION.

OH NO, YOU SEE, I *DIDN'T* BREAK ANY RULES. I DIDN'T ACT DIRECTLY AGAINST YOU.
AND WORDGIRL CAN ACT AS MY WITNESS.
UH...HE'S RIGHT.

THIS WOULDN'T HAVE HAPPENED IF YOU DIDN'T ACT SO *CORRUPT*.
AND BY *CORRUPT,* HE OBVIOUSLY MEANS UNTRUSTWORTHY AND DISLOYAL.
EXACTLY!

SEE? I TOLD YOU IT WOULD GET DEFINED EVENTUALLY.
BLAST!

AND SO ENDS ANOTHER ADVENTURE OF WORDGIRL, WHO HAD AN *EXHAUSTING* DAY FIGHTING *CORRUPT* VILLAINS, BUT FINALLY GETS THE SLEEP SHE DESERVES -- AND THE CHANCE TO DREAM OF RAINBOWS AND PONIES. WHAT A LUCKY GIRL!
AND YOU'LL BE LUCKY, TOO, IF YOU STICK AROUND FOR ANOTHER EXCITING ADVENTURE OF *WORDGIRL!*
THE END!

SUPER FANS

Chris Karwowski
WRITER

Pat Lapierre
ART

Braden Lamb
COLORS

Deron Bennett
LETTERS

BECKY AND BOB BOTSFORD ARE ENJOYING A FEW QUIET MOMENTS...
...WHILE NOT FIGHTING CRIME AS THEIR SUPER-POWERED ALTER EGOS WORDGIRL AND CAPTAIN HUGGY FACE!
3% OFF!

BUT DANGER APPEARS MORE OFTEN THAN YOU MIGHT THINK.
WHAT DO YOU THINK?

squeak!
WHOA! WHAT'S HAPPENING?

3% OFF!
THIS MALL IS BEING ROBBED. ROBBED BY ***LADY REDUNDANT WOMAN,*** LITTLE GIRL, CHILD. KID.

CAN I ASK YOU WHY YOU'RE ROBBING AN EARRING AND BRACELET STORE? IT CAN'T HAVE A LOT OF MONEY.
WE DO ALL RIGHT!
SORRY, I'M JUST NOT ***CONVINCED.***

LET'S JUST SAY...
THE BEST, GREATEST, MOST WONDERFUL PART ABOUT BEING ME IS THAT EVEN A LITTLE MONEY GOES A LONG WAY. ESPECIALLY...

...IF YOU MULTIPLY IT!
FRUIT CANAL
GASP!
eeep.

C'MON BOB, LET'S TAKE CARE OF THIS BY TURNING INTO...

WORDGIRL™
AND CAPTAIN HUGGY FACE!

HUGGY...

NICE WORK, HUGGY, LET'S TAKE THESE CLONES OUT, AND FAST.

GIVE IT UP, LADY REDUNDANT WOMAN. I WILL DEFEAT YOU, OR MY NAME ISN'T...

WORDGIRL!!!
GAH!
SUPERFANS

YOU'RE THE BEST!
I LOVE YOU, WORDGIRL!
SIGN MY AUTOGRAPH BOOK!
WAIT, YOU'RE *FANS?*

THAT'S GREAT, REALLY, BUT I'M KIND OF IN THE MIDDLE OF...UM...WHERE DID LADY REDUNDANT WOMAN GO?

OKAY, LET'S JUST BACK UP HERE A SECOND FOLKS. GIVE THE HERO SOME BREATHING ROOM.
IT'S NICE THAT YOU HOLD ME IN SUCH HIGH *ESTEEM* BUT WHAT, EXACTLY, IS GOING ON?

I CAN ANSWER THAT FOR YOU, WORDGIRL.
AS PRESIDENT OF THE INTERNATIONAL WG FAN CLUB, I INVITED ALL THESE SUPERFANS TO THE CITY FOR THE FIRST EVER WORDGIRL CONVENTION.
TJ?

IT SEEMS THAT THE SUPERFANS NOW HOLD ***YOU*** IN HIGH ***ESTEEM.***
YES... ***ESTEEM***...I TOTALLY KNOW WHAT THAT MEANS.
DO YOU WANT ME TO DEFINE IT FOR YOU?

DEFINE IT!
DEFINE IT!
DEFINE IT!
UH... OKAAAAAY.

ESTEEM IS A FAVORABLE OPINION OF SOMEONE OR SOMETHING.
TO HOLD SOMEONE IN HIGH ESTEEM IS TO RESPECT THEM A LOT.

YAAYYYYY!
THIS IS WEIRD, HUGGY.

SO, WHAT IS GOING ON?
WHO ARE THESE PEOPLE?
OUTSIDE OF *ME,* THESE PEOPLE ARE YOUR BIGGEST FANS.
THEY ARE YOUR SUPERFANS AND WE'RE HERE TO CELEBRATE ALL THINGS WORDGIRL!

WHO ARE *THEY?*
OH, THAT'S THE CAPTAIN HUGGY FACE FAN CLUB. THEY'RE NOT PART OF THE OFFICIAL WORDGIRL CONVENTION BUT WE'RE LETTING THEM TAG ALONG.

eee!
HE SAW US! *HE SAW US!*
THIS IS THE *GREATEST* DAY OF MY LIFE!

WE SHOULD GO. TJ, DO YOU WANT A LIFT HOME?
IT'S ABOUT DINNERTIME AND MOM, UH, I MEAN *YOUR MOTHER* GETS UPSET WHEN YOU OR YOUR SISTER BECKY ARE LATE.

YES! I'LL FLY WITH YOU, WORDGIRL! AGAIN!
WELL, YOU'RE NOT HARD TO *CONVINCE...*

SO, WORDGIRL. HOW DO YOU LIKE THE SUPERFAN CONVENTION?
IT'S NICE TO KNOW THAT SO MANY PEOPLE HOLD ME IN HIGH *ESTEEM.* BUT, TO BE HONEST, THEY KIND OF DISTRACTED ME FROM CATCHING LADY REDUNDANT WOMAN.
DON'T WORRY, I'M SURE YOU'LL DO BETTER NEXT TIME.

NEXT TIME!? TJ, I THINK...
OH, THAT'S MY HOUSE.
SO IT IS.

LATER, AT THE BOTSFORD RESIDENCE, BECKY AND BOB...
AND THEN, LADY REDUNDANT WOMAN COMES OUT OF THE MALL, FOLLOWED BY WORDGIRL, WHO WAS SO STUNNED TO SEE ME SHE LET LADY REDUNDANT WOMAN GET AWAY.
WHAT!?

AND THEN WORDGIRL OFFERED TO FLY ME BACK TO MY HOUSE, WHERE SHE TOLD ME I WAS HER BIGGEST, BESTEST SUPERFAN.
WOW. SOUNDS LIKE A FULL DAY, CHAMP.
HONEY, I'M SO PROUD YOUR CONVENTION IS GOING SO WELL.
WORDGIRL WOULD NEVER SAY THAT.

HOW WOULD YOU KNOW, BECKY?! YOU WEREN'T EVEN THERE.
I JUST KNOW WORDGIRL, AND SHE WOULDN'T SAY THAT.

WELL SHE DIDN'T SAY IT EXACTLY. SHE SAID IT WITH HER EYES.
OH BROTHER.

THE NEXT DAY, WORDGIRL AND HUGGY GO IN SEARCH OF LADY REDUNDANT WOMAN...
ACTUALLY, HUGGY, I REALLY *LIKE* THE SUPERFANS. I JUST THINK IT'S GOING TO GET OUT OF CONTROL AND GO TO TJ'S HEAD.
COOS.
HOW CAN I BE SURE?
WORLD'S LONGEST STRIP MALL

DOES *THAT CONVINCE* YOU?
HELLO WORDGIRL!

WHAT IS GOING ON?
ISN'T THIS GREAT?
THE SUPERFANS WERE SO IMPRESSED THAT YOU FLEW ME HOME THAT THEY TOLD ME THEY WOULD DO ANYTHING I WANTED.
SO I HAD EVERYONE DRESS UP LIKE WORDGIRL AND CARRY ME AROUND ALL DAY.
IS THIS HOW YOU TREAT PEOPLE WHO HOLD YOU IN HIGH *ESTEEM?*

I'LL DEAL WITH YOU LATER.

SO, WORDGIRL, IT APPEARS YOU HAVE GATHERED YOURSELF AN ARMY, A SQUAD, AND A PLATOON.

ARMY? NO, THESE ARE...
UH... I MEAN, YEAH.

I *DO* HAVE AN ARMY, SO YOU BETTER JUST BACK DOWN WITHOUT FIGHTING ME AND MY EQUALLY POWERFUL ARMY OF WORDGIRL CLONES.

NO, I DON'T THINK I WILL. *COPIES...*

ADVANCE! CHARGE! ATTACK!
WAIT...

OK, FINE, SO THEY'RE NOT REALLY MY CLONES. LET THEM GO!
I CAN'T BELIEVE I'M BEING HELD HOSTAGE BY A REAL VILLAIN.
I KNOW! SUPER EXCITING!

DID YOU THINK THAT THEY WOULD FOOL, CON, AND OUTFOX ME WITH THESE COSTUMES?
MAYBE?

BUT I GUESS THE QUESTION IS WHAT DO WE DO NOW? YOU CAN'T ATTACK ME WITHOUT YOUR FANS GETTING HURT. BUT IF I LET THEM GO, WHAT'S TO STOP YOU FROM ATTACKING ME?
WE COULD JUST AGREE TO NOT FIGHT.

NO, I DON'T THINK SO.
WOW, YOU DON'T HOLD ME IN VERY HIGH *ESTEEM.*

DOES THAT ALWAYS HAPPEN WHEN YOU FIGHT LADY REDUNDANT WOMAN?
HOW DID YOU MEET CAPTAIN HUGGY FACE?
HOW DO YOU THINK OF YOUR SECRET PLANS?

TJ, I'D LIKE TO TALK TO YOU.
SURE THING, WORDGIRL.

TJ, THIS HAS TO STOP. YOU ARE PUTTING THESE PEOPLE IN DANGER.
BUT THEY LOVE SEEING YOU IN ACTION.

AND HOW IS IT THAT YOU'VE BEEN ABLE TO FIND ME SO FAST?

SOME OF THE SUPERFANS BUILT A LOW-ORBITING SATELLITE WHOSE SOLE JOB IS TO FIND YOU.

TJ, I REALLY THINK...
SUPERFANS, CUT DOWN WORDGIRL. I'LL GO GET THE TRIVIA CONTEST READY.
THANKS, WORDGIRL!

BUT...
WORDGIRL, PLEASE HOLD STILL. WE ONLY HAVE ONE PAIR OF SCISSORS AND IT'S VERY DULL.

CAN I HAVE A PICTURE WITH YOU?
WHO ARE YOUR FAVORITE 20 VILLAINS, FROM BEST TO WORST?
CAN YOU TAKE ME FOR A RIDE? FLY AROUND THE CITY?
THAT'S PERFECT.

ONE LONG CUTTING-DOWN, PICTURE-TAKING EVENT LATER.
WOW, INDOOR MALL, STRIP MALL AND NOW OUTDOOR MALL. LADY REDUNDANT WOMAN SURE LIKES TO KEEP ON THEME.

AND HERE ARE THE SUPERFANS.

HI GUYS, I'M ACTUALLY GLAD TO SEE ALL OF YOU.
REALLY?
REALLY.

AFTER YOU CUT US DOWN, HUGGY AND I CAME UP WITH A PLAN TO DEFEAT LADY REDUNDANT WOMAN, BUT WE NEED ALL YOUR HELP.

TOBY VANCE
BOY SINGING SENSATION
YOU SEE, WE WERE THINKING...
IT'S TOBY VANCE!

HEY! WHAT KIND OF FAIR-WEATHER FANS ARE YOU?

I'M SORRY WORDGIRL. I THOUGHT THEY WERE TRUE FANS.
THAT'S OKAY, TJ.

I'M GLAD *YOU'RE* STILL A LOYAL SUPERFAN.
PLUS HUGGY'S FANS ARE STILL HERE.

BEING LOYAL IS A HUGE PART OF BEING A CAPTAIN HUGGY FACE FAN.
THAT'S SO SWEET! BUT NOW I'M NOT *CONVINCED* THAT WE HAVE ENOUGH PEOPLE FOR OUR PLAN.

COMING UP WITH PLANS ON THE SPOT IS ANOTHER PART OF BEING INSPIRED BY CAPTAIN HUGGY FACE.
HE DOESN'T HAVE SUPERPOWERS YET HE ALWAYS COMES UP WITH A WAY TO HELP.
AWWWW...SO TRUE. WHAT'S YOUR IDEA?

HALT YOUR CRIME SPREE, LADY REDUNDANT WOMAN!

NO WAY, WORDGIRL! BESIDES WHO'S GOING TO STOP ME?

THIS ARMY!

AHHH!
I CAN'T SEE! TOMATO JUICE IN MY EYE!

POP!
POP!
POP!
POP!

SO, LADY REDUNDANT WOMAN. DO I HAVE TO *CONVINCE* YOU TO GIVE UP NOW?
I DON'T UNDERSTAND WHAT THAT MEANS. I'M CONFUSED. PUZZLED. STUMPED.

TO *CONVINCE* SOMEONE, YOU HAVE TO GIVE AN ARGUMENT THAT PERSUADES THEM TO FOLLOW YOUR COURSE OF ACTION.

INTERESTING, BUT I DON'T THINK I'LL BE *CONVINCED* TO GIVE MYSELF UP.

BUT I WAS PAYING ATTENTION WHEN YOU BLINDED MY COPIES!
ACK!

SO LONG, WORDGIRL!

CAPTAIN HUGGY FACE FANS! ***ASSEMBLE!***

DRAT! CURSES! OUCH!

HIYA!

WOW! GOOD JOB, GUYS.
THIS IS PRETTY MUCH THE BEST DAY OF MY LIFE.

TJ, WHY DON'T YOU HAND OVER THAT REMOTE CONTROL?
AW MAN.

FIND WORDGIRL
SELF DESTRUCT

I TOLD THEM THAT BUTTON WASN'T A GOOD IDEA.
C'MON. I CAN FLY YOU HOME AGAIN.
WOW! REALLY?

BEING A WORDGIRL FAN IS THE BEST!!
AND SO CONCLUDES ANOTHER EXCITING EPISODE OF WORDGIRL. YOU'LL NEVER CONVINCE ME THAT READERS WON'T HOLD THIS ADVENTURE IN HIGH ESTEEM. KEEP READING FOR ANOTHER UNBELIEVABLE TALE IN THE NEXT ISSUE OF WORDGIRL!
THE END

GLOSSARY

Exhausted [ig-zaws-ted]

To drain of strength or energy, wear out, or fatigue greatly, as a person.

Coalition [koh-uh-lish-uhn]

A combination or alliance, especially a temporary one between persons, factions, states, etc.

Malice [mal-is]

Desire to inflict injury, harm, or suffering on another, either because of a hostile impulse or out of deep-seated meanness.

Professional [pruh-fesh-uh-nl]

Following an occupation as a means of livelihood or for gain.

Amateur [am-uh-choor]

A person inexperienced or unskilled in a particular activity.

Confused [kuhn-fyoozd]

Perplexed or bewildered.

Innocent [in-uh-suhnt]

Not involving evil intent or motive.

Corrupt [kuh-ruhpt]

Guilty of dishonest practices, as bribery; lacking integrity.

Convinced [kuhn-vinced]

To move by argument or evidence to belief, agreement, consent, or a course of action.

Multiply [muhl-tuh-plahy]

To make many or manifold.

Clones [klohn]

A cell, cell product, or organism that is genetically identical to the unit or individual from which it was derived.

Autograph [aw-tuh-graf, -grahf]

Something written in a person's own hand, as a manuscript or letter.

Esteem [ih-steem]

To regard highly or favorably; regard with respect or admiration.

Convention [kuhn-ven-shuhn]

A meeting or formal assembly, as of representatives or delegates, for discussion of and action on particular matters of common concern.

Distracted [dih-strak-tid]

Having the attention diverted.

Stunned [stuhn-d]

To deprive of consciousness or strength by or as if by a blow, fall, etc.

Impressed [im-pres-d]

To affect deeply or strongly in mind or feelings; influence in opinion.

Satellite [sat-l-ahyt]

A minor structure accompanying a more important or larger one.

Inspired [in-spahyuhrd]

To fill with an animating, quickening, or exalting influence.